Puppy love! Ellen & Ernie

Written by
Ellen Sinaiko
with Ernestine

illustrated by
Cristina Ghelfi

This book belongs to

· — · — · — · — · — · — · — ·

..cut out a little
picture of puppy's face
and glue it here!

FIRST EDITION

All rights reserved, including the right of
reproduction in whole or in part in any form.

Copyright © 1996 by Ellen Sinaiko and Ernestine Sinaiko

Published by Vantage Press, Inc.
516 West 34th Street, New York, New York 10001

Manufactured in the United States of America
ISBN: 0-533-11743-7

Library of Congress Catalog Card No.: 95-90861

0 9 8 7 6 5 4

Wishing you Joy and Happiness on your new one!

Here's to all the dogs,
the large and the small
who bring so much love,
happiness and devotion
to all.

This book is dedicated to Ernestine

Special unconditional thanks to Cristina Ghelfi and Carla Glasser

Puppy Arrives

Date of birth

Weight

Height

Length

Color of eyes

Puppy looks like

On the day you arrived mother
and father were

Puppy came from

Family history

First Photographs

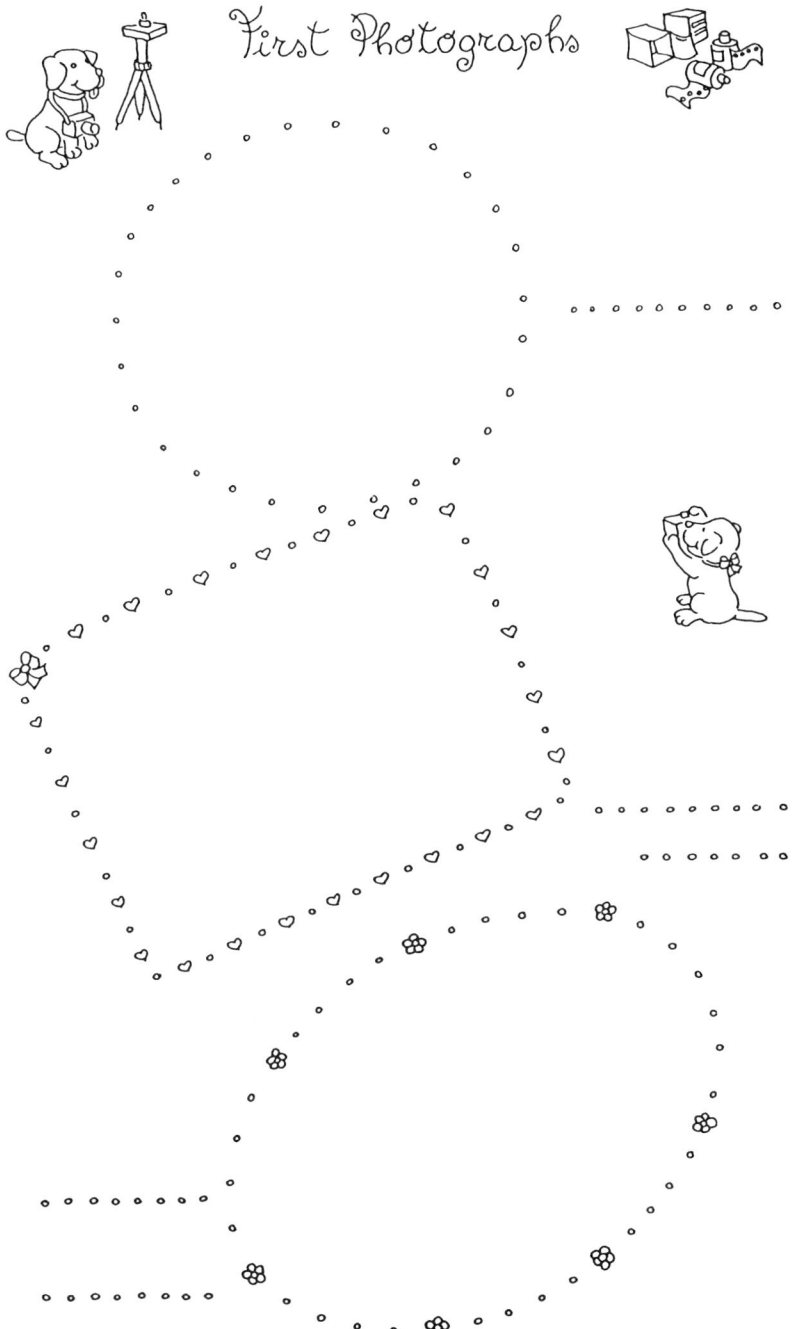

Puppy's Name

On the   day of

Our puppy was named

Named for

Godmother

Godfather

Those present

Place photograph here

Record of Growth

Age	Weight	Height	Length
one month	_____	_____	_____
two months	_____	_____	_____
three months	_____	_____	_____
four months	_____	_____	_____
five months	_____	_____	_____
six months	_____	_____	_____
seven months	_____	_____	_____
eight months	_____	_____	_____
nine months	_____	_____	_____
ten months	_____	_____	_____
eleven months	_____	_____	_____
one year	_____	_____	_____
two years	_____	_____	_____
three years	_____	_____	_____

Favorite Notes and Letters of Congratulations

Paste letters here

Favorite Gifts

Item	From whom	Puppy's reaction
_____	_____	_____
_____	_____	_____
_____	_____	_____
_____	_____	_____
_____	_____	_____
_____	_____	_____
_____	_____	_____
_____	_____	_____
_____	_____	_____
_____	_____	_____

Astrologically Barking

Zodiac sign

Birthstone

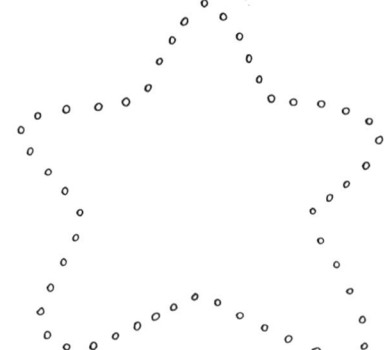

Flower

♡ # Spiritual and Religious Ceremonies and Celebrations ♡

Place Record of First Exam Here

First Veterinarian Exam

At puppy's first visit to the doctor:

Weight

Length

The doctor said

Vet's name

Address

Phone number

A puppy needs several days to adjust to a new home. Try to bring the puppy home on a weekend. Make sure you are prepared and have proper food, water, sleeping area, collar, leash and a safe area for puppy to call his own.

Place photograph here of puppy at home

Puppy's First Home

Address _____

Phone number _____

Special preparations _____
_____

Behavior of puppy _____
_____

First visitors _____
_____

First surprises _____
_____

Tender first moments _____
_____
_____

Picture of home here

Homemade Puppy Chow

1 cup regular hamburger
1 cup brown rice
1/4 cup carrots (minced)

Prepare rice according to directions on the package. Mix rice, hamburger and carrots in a bowl. Bake at 350 degrees until brown. Serve cooled.

Feeding Habits

Date puppy first:

Ate puréed food

Ate puppy chow

Begged for people food

Ate something that was **not** food

Ate street food covered with ants

Discovered steak tartare

Barking Development

First time puppy:

Squeaked

Barked

Growled at another dog

Barked to go outside

Howled at a fire engine

Sang to music
and
did not forget the words

Barked **"I Love You"**

Puppy Talk

Barking is natural and a dog that barks at strange noises or unexpected visitors should not be punished but praised. Problem barking is when it is a disturbance. To stop this behavior:

*Give a firm "**NO**"*
Distract dog with a toy
Exercise more
Offer a treat
*Leave the **TV** or radio on*
*Hire a "**TRAINER!**"*

Place photograph here

 # Puppy Sleeps

Bedtimes

Places to sleep

Discovers your bed
and
sleeps with you

Favorite sleeping positions

Sleeps in your lap

Sleeps through the night
and
let's you sleep through the night

Favorite lullabies

Has **"puppy dreams"**

Sweet Dreams

*It is
important
that puppies
have
sufficient
sleep.*
Most puppies
need
at least
ten hours
a night
and naps
during
the day.

Place photograph of puppy sleeping here

Puppy's First Bath

Groomer

Date

Details of puppy's reaction

Place first lock here

Puppy's First Tooth

First tooth lost

What the tooth fairy left

Place first tooth in
an envelope here

Personal Habits

Describe when puppy first:

Understood paper training

Was housebroken

Barked to go out

Drank from the toilet bowl

*Favorite housebreaking **horror** story*
_____
_____
_____
_____
_____

Ernie's Favorite Flea Treatment

2 tablespoons of cider vinegar
1 cup of dry skin lotion
3 tablespoons of a natural insect repellent
1 cup water

Put above ingredients in a 16-ounce spray bottle and shake until mixed. Rub into dog's coat.

Favorite Things

Chew toys

Cuddly toys

Objects

Games

Activities

Sounds

Songs

People

Hiding places

Places to dig holes

Homemade Toy

Canvas fabric

Old socks or T-shirt

Heavy-duty thread and needle

Cut folded canvas in half so you have two alike pieces. Cut into your favorite shape. Hand sew or use a machine to stitch pieces together. Leave a small unstitched space. Turn sewn piece inside out. Cut socks or T-shirt into small pieces and stuff to fill out shape. Hand sew the open space tightly, making sure there are no loose spaces or threads.

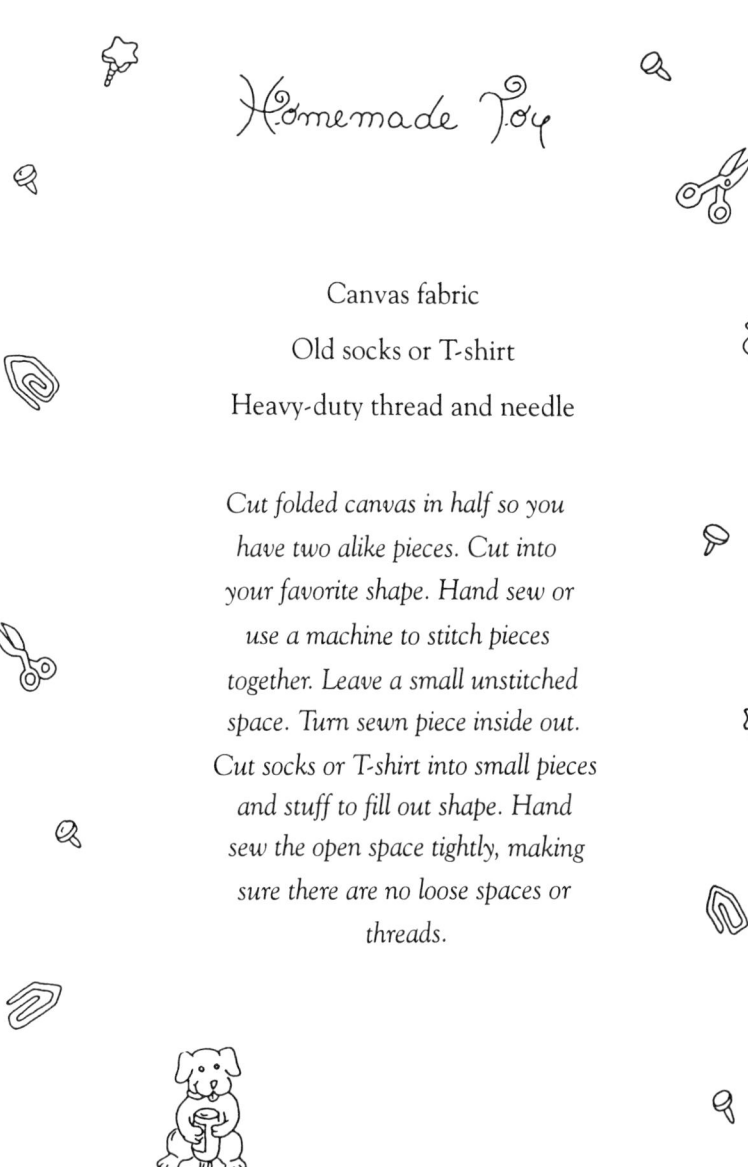

First Outings

Details of first trips:

Car

Airplane

Train

Boat

Outings to:

Grandparents

Special friends

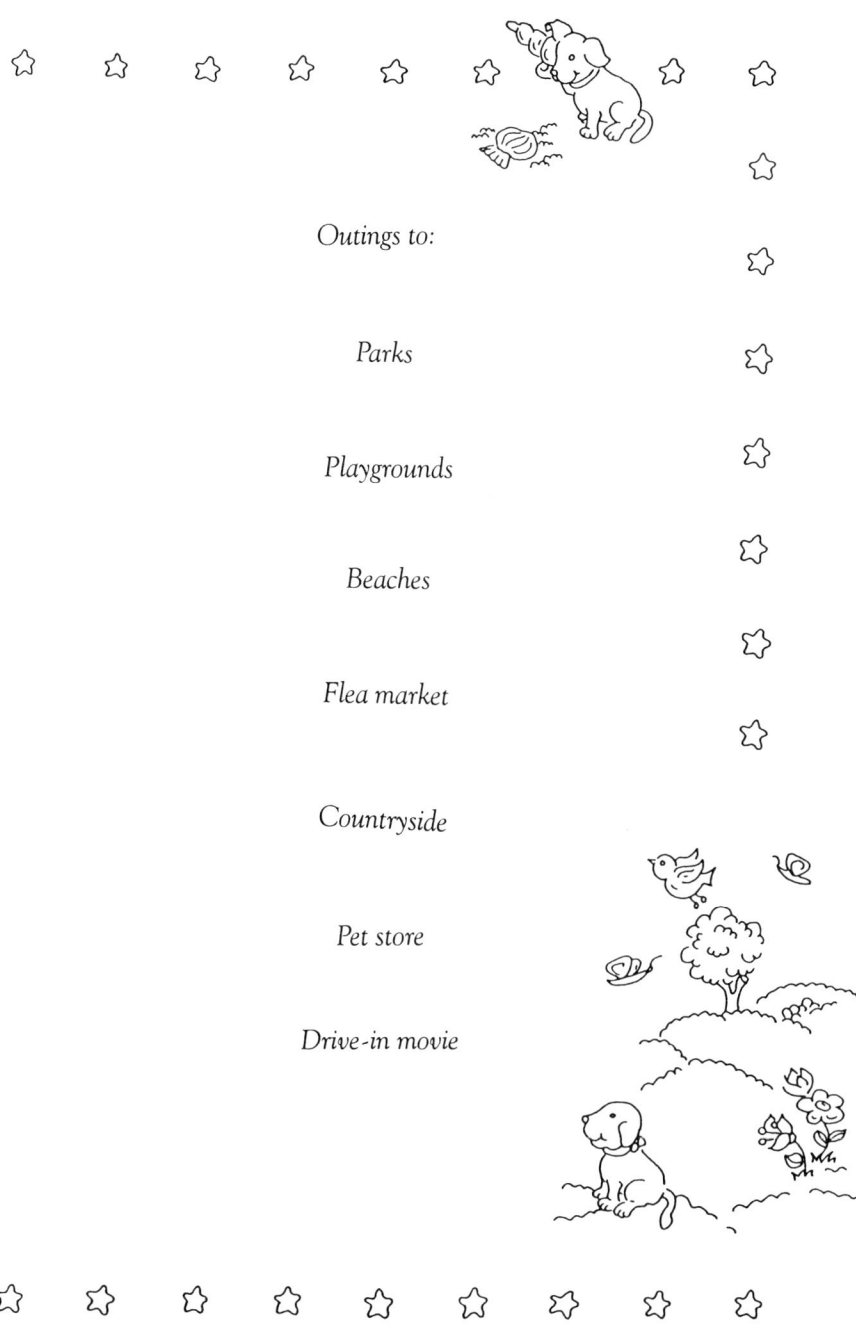

Outings to:

Parks

Playgrounds

Beaches

Flea market

Countryside

Pet store

Drive-in movie

Character Development

First rolls over

First smile

First grasps a toy with paws

First sits up

First fetches the morning paper
and
does **not** eat it

First kiss

First plays a joke

First encounter with a squirrel

First discovers something disgusting
and
rolls in it

Funny Bones

Details of silly things puppy does!

Place photograph here

What a Silly Puppy

School Days

Name of school

Date of entrance

Problems

Favorite classmates

Favorite teacher

Teacher's comments

_____
_____
_____
_____

Place report card here

Mother and Father Notes

My puppy is a genius!

Place favorite
photograph here

First Evening Out Without Puppy

Details of evening!

Mother Nature

Seasons • Weather • Animals • Plants

Actions Pertaining To Sex

It's time to discuss the birds and the bees!

Place photograph here

Most Embarrassing Moments

That's not my puppy!

Place photograph here

Favorite Restaurants

Restaurant	Description of meal
_____	_____
_____	_____
_____	_____
_____	_____
_____	_____
_____	_____

Place doggie bag here

Ernie's Mock People Treats

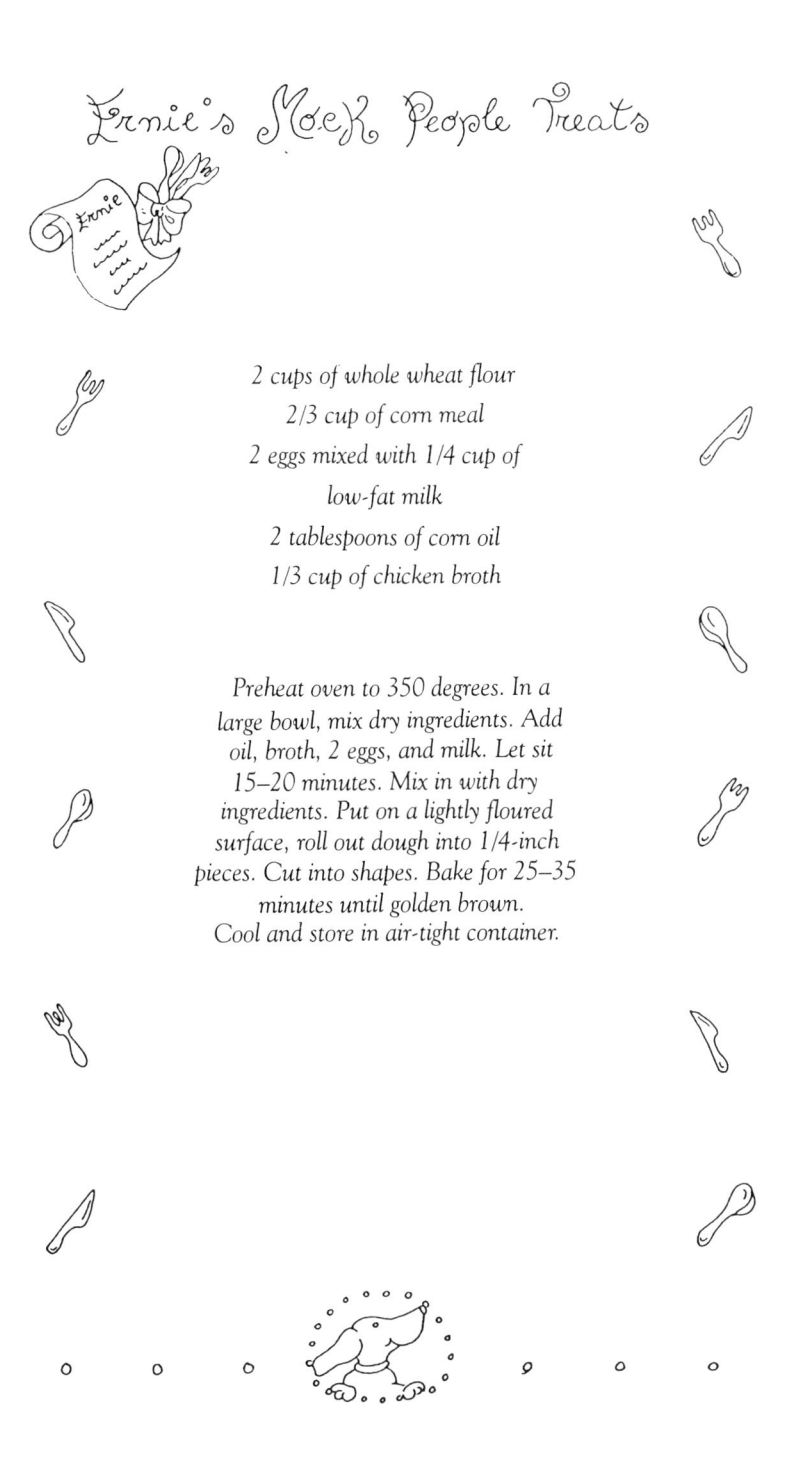

2 cups of whole wheat flour
2/3 cup of corn meal
2 eggs mixed with 1/4 cup of
low-fat milk
2 tablespoons of corn oil
1/3 cup of chicken broth

Preheat oven to 350 degrees. In a large bowl, mix dry ingredients. Add oil, broth, 2 eggs, and milk. Let sit 15–20 minutes. Mix in with dry ingredients. Put on a lightly floured surface, roll out dough into 1/4-inch pieces. Cut into shapes. Bake for 25–35 minutes until golden brown.
Cool and store in air-tight container.

One Year Old

How celebrated

Who was there

Description of cake

Gifts received

_____
_____
_____
_____
_____

Place photograph here

How We Survived Puppy Days

What Did Not Survive Puppy Days

Paste piece of
surviving remnant
here

Holiday Celebrations

Occasions

Gifts

Traditions

Place photograph here

Dates

Friends

Holiday Celebrations

♡ Occasions

♡ Gifts

♡ Dates

Place photograph here

♡ Traditions

♡ Friends

Family Album

Favorite photographs

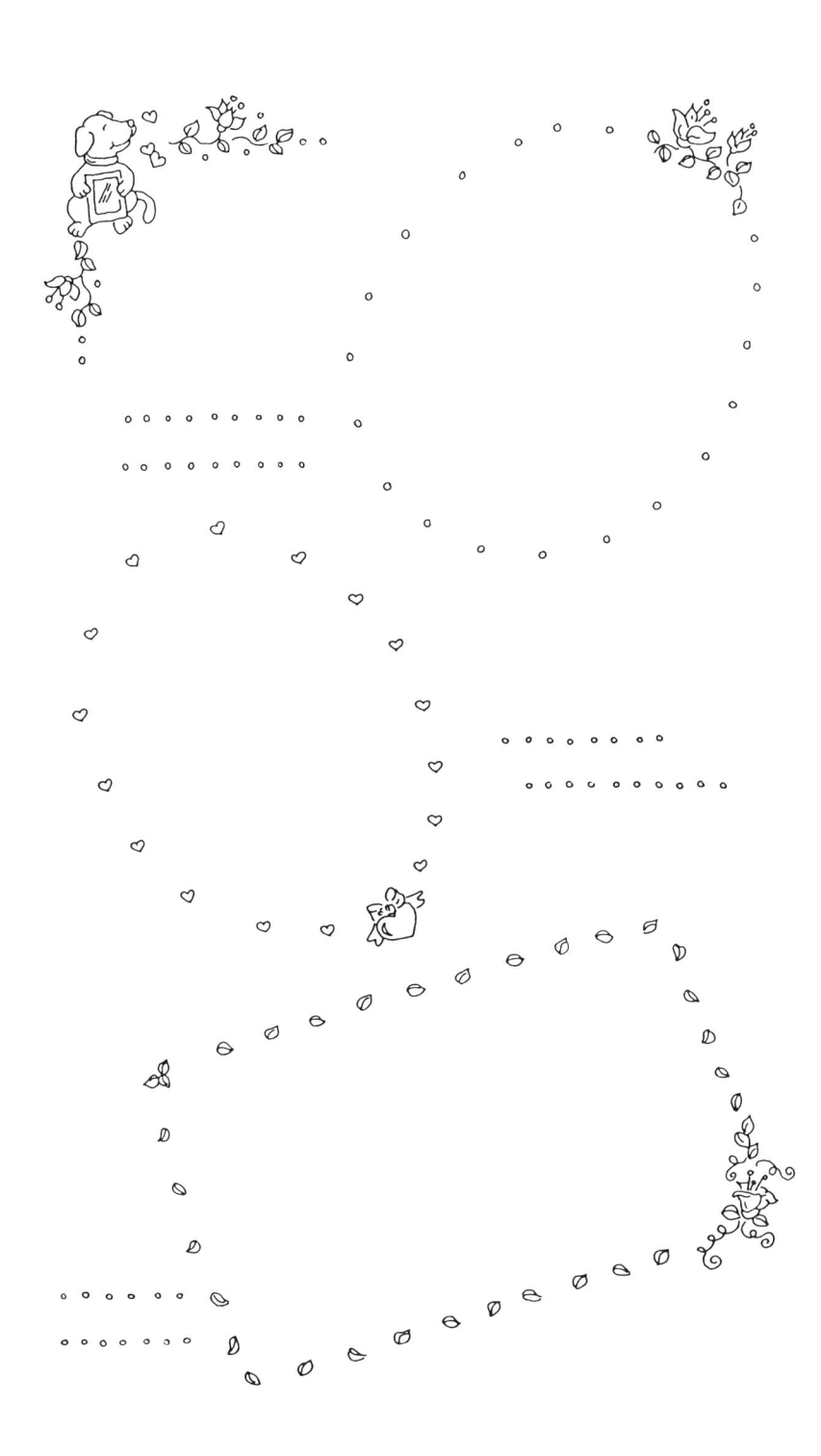